CAN U SAVE THE DAY?

Written by SHANNON STOCKER

Illustrated by TOM DISBURY

The letter **A** sat by a frog
and chatted with a duck and dog
until the letter **B** swept by,
a wicked twinkle in his eye.

"There are **5** vowels in your group but **21** in our grand troop. I'm a more important letter. Consonants are so... much... BETTER!"

A knew it only took one hand to count the members in her band.

But consonants need all the toes and all the fingers PLUS a nose.

The letter **B** stuck out his tongue
and bragged, "Our group is **#1**!"
Offended, **A** said, "You'll regret
when all the **vowels** are gone, I bet."

Then **POOF!** Like that, **A** disappeared!

That's when things got a little weird.

brk!
brk!

Instead of bark,
the dog said **"brk."**

quck?

And the duck couldn't quack,
she could only **"quck."**

And the frog? Poor thing. He couldn't croak.
He could only **"crok,"** that woeful bloke.

crok

The horse laughed, "Neigh! Who needs the **A**?"

And turned his back to eat some hay.

But then **E** said, "I'm going, too.
You're being rude. I don't like you."

So **E** took off. Things went awry,

and all the horse could say was "nigh!"

The birds sang "twt" instead of tweet,

and the sheep just "blt" instead of bleat.

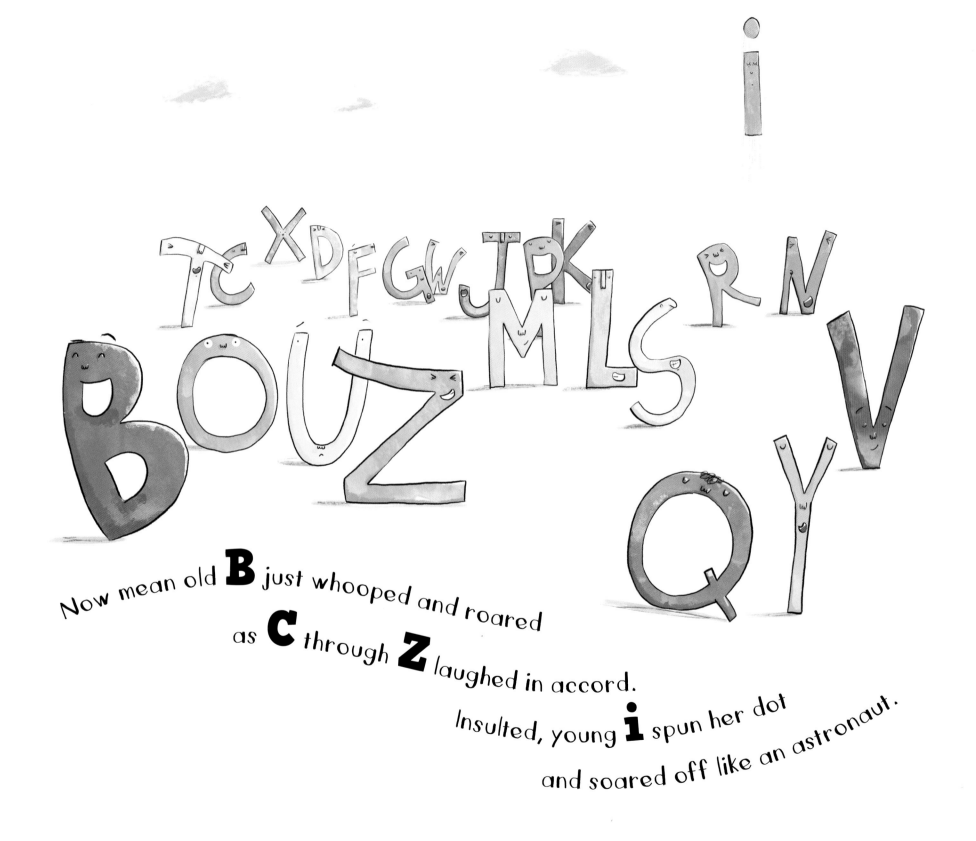

Now mean old **B** just whooped and roared
as **C** through **Z** laughed in accord.
Insulted, young **i** spun her dot
and soared off like an astronaut.

Turning back, she waved goodbye
and the horse just hung his head to cry.

"Ngh!" was all that he could utter.

Ngh!

Onk!

"Onk!" was all the pig could mutter.

The cow cracked up beside the bunny—
they thought it was all too funny,
so they sat and watched the fun

as **A**, **E**, **i** left, one by one.

But wouldn't you know, the next to go
would be the cow's lone vowel, **O**?

Mmmmmm

"Mmmmmm" was all that she could say
when **O** decided not to stay.

C

The pigeons, too, they couldn't coo!
"C" was all that they could do.

cck-ddl-d

And Rooster? I bet you can guess—
"cck-ddl-d," he said, distressed.

The consonants were so absorbed

in laughing that they all ignored

a tractor speeding toward their crowd.

Fast asleep, ahead it plowed!

Only **U** and **B** observed

the tractor as it swung and swerved.

Zzzzzzzzz ...

it snoozed and snored away,

gaining speed, to **B**'s dismay!

STOP!

B tried to shout, in fear.

But "stp!" was all the world could hear.

stp!

And when he tried to scream

WATCH OUT!

"wtch ut" was all that he could spout.

wtch ut!

Determined, **B** jumped to his feet
and vaulted to the tractor's seat.
This was a test **B** couldn't flunk!
B pushed the horn! The horn went...

hnk.

hnk

So no one heard.

No one cared.

B turned to **U**, a plea prepared.

But vowel-less, words wouldn't flow,

so **B**'s unease began to grow.

Calmly, **U** held up her hand.
She could make **B** understand
that yes, indeed, their group was small
but with no vowels, words will stall.

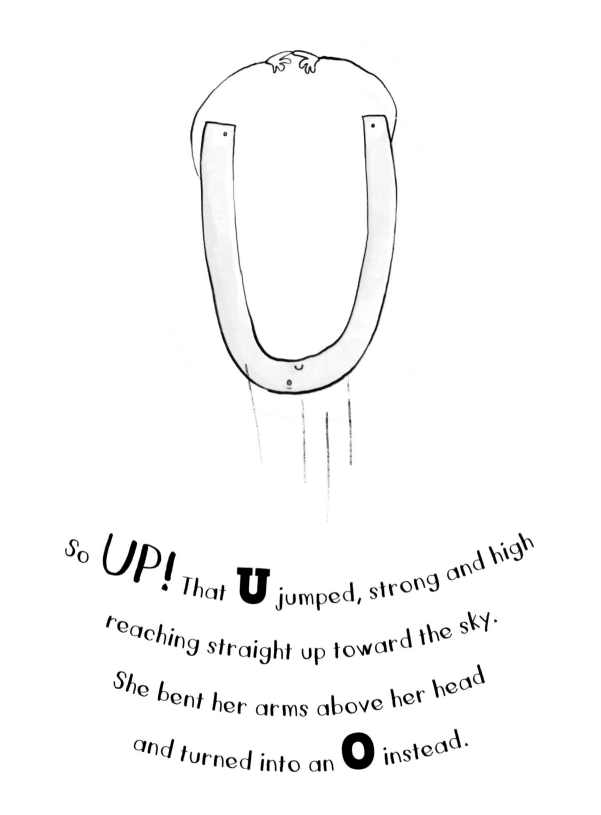

So **UP!** That **U** jumped, strong and high reaching straight up toward the sky. She bent her arms above her head and turned into an **O** instead.

When she did, that horn could sound—

HONK! The warning shook the ground.

The tractor woke with the alert

and stopped in time.

No one was hurt.

HONK!

U turned toward the consonants,
nodded with some confidence,
and off she marched to make things right
and help the letters reunite.

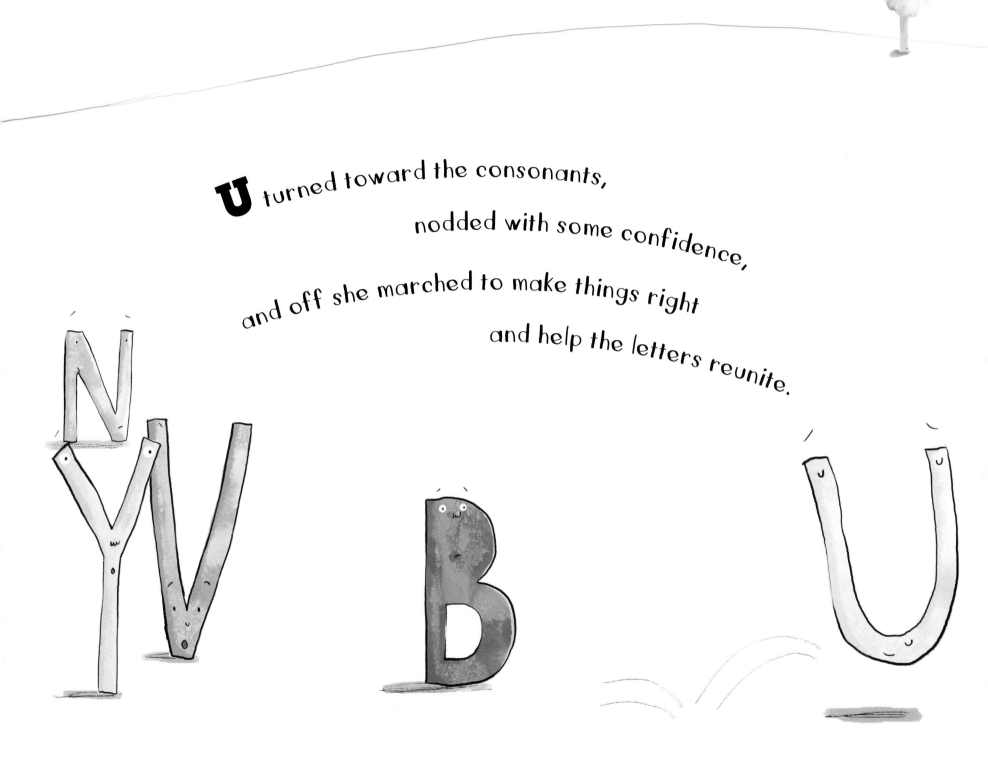

Once **A E I O U** came back,

the dog could **bark,**

the duck could **quack,**

the frog could **croak,**

the birds could **tweet,**

the horse could **neigh,**

the sheep could **bleat**,

the pig could **oink**,

the cow could **moo**,

the tractor **honk**,

the pigeons **coo**.

And what about the rooster?

Yeah.

He too could **cock-a-doodle-doodle-doo**.

Sheepishly, the letters shrugged.

The consonants and vowels hugged.

B said, "Sorry. Now we see

the alphabet's a family."

Then, a steady voice said, "Wait!

I have one thing that I must state.

At times, I feel left out," said **Y**.

"But you need me

to

say

GOODBYE!"

For G, C, and T—without whom
my alphabet would be incomplete.

—S

😄

For Mum and Dad

—T

Sleeping Bear Press®
2395 South Huron Parkway, Suite 200
Ann Arbor, MI 48104
www.sleepingbearpress.com

Printed and bound in the United States.

10 9 8 7 6 5 4 3 2 1

Library of Congress Cataloging-in-Publication Data

Names: Stocker, Shannon, author. | Disbury, Tom, illustrator.
Title: Can U save the day? / by Shannon Stocker ; illustrated by Tom Disbury.
Description: Ann Arbor, MI : Sleeping Bear Press, [2019] | Summary: B picks
on the vowels, because their numbers are so small, while other consonants laugh,
but when the vowels disappear one by one, only U can set things right.
Identifiers: LCCN 2019009903 | ISBN 9781585364046 (hardcover)
Subjects: | CYAC: Stories in rhyme. | Alphabet—Fiction. | Bullying—Fiction.
Classification: LCC PZ8.3.S8654 Can 2019 | DDC [E]—dc23
LC record available at https://lccn.loc.gov/2019009903

A B C D E F G H I J K L M N O P Q R S T U V W X Y Z